D1429964

Dedication

Thank you Abby and Josh for inspiring me to be brave and 'Dream Big'. Love you both!

Joshua Cleans Up!

by Laura Yeva

Illustrated by Yekaterina Likhovidova

A CIP catalogue record for this title is available from the British Library.

ISBN 9781786936486 (Paperback)
ISBN 9781786936493 (Hardback)
ISBN 9781786936509 (E-Book)
www.austinmacauley.com

First Published (2017)
Austin Macauley Publishers Ltd.
25 Canada Square
Canary Wharf
London
E14 5LQ

ABOUT JOSHUA

When my little Josh was born, he was a joy in my life immediately. He loved life, he was all smiles and showed so much interest for knowledge. He wanted to learn and made everything look easy.

Books were his first love, then came the toys that go. Cars, trucks, trains were on his mind a lot.

When the Disney movie 'Cars' came out, Josh fell in love with Lightning McQueen. All he wanted to do was drive fast like a race car. He used to tell us, "If I can't drive a race car, I will be a race car!"

Early in the morning Joshua wakes up.

He calls, "Papa, Papa, Milk!"
Then he says, "Mama, Mama, Books!"

Mama and Papa pick him up from his crib and they kiss him and hug him.

"Good morning baby!"

"How did you sleep my Joshi?
We love you very much!"
say Mommy and Daddy.

Joshua smiles, and hugs and kisses his mama and papa.
This means that he had a good night's sleep.

Josh adores books!
And his favorite cow MOO-MOO loves reading
books too.

He has fun reading with his daddy.

After Joshi drinks milk and reads books, he runs
to his room to play with his toys.

He does not forget his MOO-MOO,
she is Special!

Joshua plays with blocks, cars, trains,
soft animals, trucks, and many other toys.

His imagination is Big!
He imagines that he is a sailor, a conductor, and a
race car driver.

His toys are everywhere.
In the living room,
in the bedroom, and in the kitchen.

Wow, Josh knows how to play very well!

Mama says, "Please clean up Joshua. You need to put your toys away if you are done playing with them."

Little Josh listens to Mommy and starts to gather up his blocks into the block box.
He is being a good boy!

He puts his cars and trains away into the big
Lightning McQueen box.
Joshua knows where everything goes.
EXCELLENT!

He puts his soft animals away, they go on the top of the couch and on the windowsill. He wants Mommy to praise him and he waits for Mommy's attention.

"**Wow Joshua**, what a super fantastic job you have done! You are great at cleaning your room, and that is a big help for Mama!" says Mommy happily.

In the afternoon Mommy and Josh have lunch together.

They enjoy each other's company.
Josh does not forget to feed his MOO-MOO,
she loves salad!

After lunch, it is nap time!

He loves reading books before nap time.
Mama reads to Joshua a couple of books that
he has chosen on his own.

One of his favorite books is 'Goodnight Moon'.
He is all ready for his nap.
"Have a great nap my baby Josh," Mommy tucks
him in.

Here comes Josh again, after his nap, he starts to play with all of his toys at the same time.

"You are playing so nicely, you are my sweet boy!" says his mom.
Josh loves playing with dinosaurs.

"If you want to go outside before dinner Josh, please tidy up your room."
Joshua gladly cleans up. He is happy to go outside.
"Thank you! We will go to the park," says Mommy.

Mama praised him.
"Excellent work, you are my huge help!
I love you, you are my happy boy!"
says mommy affectionately.

"I love you too, my Princess Mommy!"
says Josh.

Joshua has been Good all day.

At night time, he says good night to his room,
to his blocks, to his cars, to his trains,
to his books,
and to all of his soft toys.

Josh went to sleep after drinking his
warm milk and after
Daddy read him his favorite books.

He took his MOO-MOO with him to bed,
because Joshi never goes to sleep without
his favorite friend.

"Goodnight!"

"You are such a good boy. I love everything about you. You are my Sweet Chocolate Chip Cookie!" says his loving mommy.

"Tomorrow is a new day and we will do everything all over again. But now, you need to close your eyes and sleep," Mommy says softly.

Mommy sings to Josh:
"Hush, Hush, Time to Sleep
Say Goodnight, Close Your Eyes
Fall Asleep, Sleep Tight."

"Goodnight my boy. I am proud of you!
You are a big help for Mama.
You are my little buddy and a soldier.
Sweet dreams!
I love you!" says Daddy to Josh.

See you again soon!